Doctor Kangaroo

Gerald Hawksley

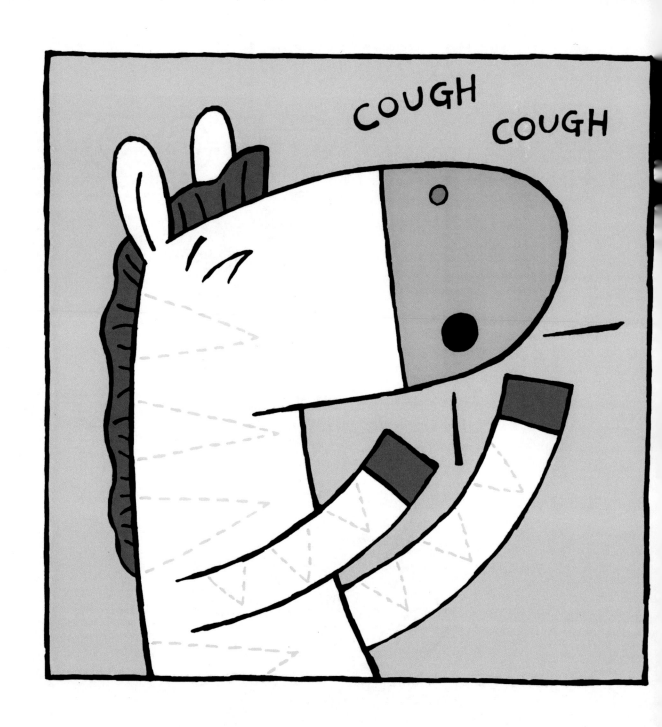

Zebra has a cough.
All his stripes have fallen off.

Crocodile has lost his snap.
He's not a happy chap.

Parrot's bent her beak.
She can hardly speak.

What are we going to do?
Call for Doctor Kangaroo!

Doctor Kangaroo says,
"Get to bed!
Put a bandage on your head!
You'll be better in a day.
Now I must be on my way!"

Hippo's looking glum.
He has a poorly tum.

Snake has lost his slither.
He can't go hither, or go thither.

Elephant doesn't feel too hot.
His trunk is tied into a knot.

What are we going to do?
Call for Doctor Kangaroo!

Doctor Kangaroo says,
"Get to bed!
Put a bandage on your head!
You'll soon be right as rain.
You won't need to call for me again."

Lion's hurt his paw.
It's really rather sore.

Monkey's ears are itchy.
He is cross and twitchy.

Giraffe is in a tizzy.
She's feeling sick and dizzy.

What are we going to do?
Call for Doctor Kangaroo!

Doctor Kangaroo says,
"Get to bed!
Put a bandage on your head!
That's what you need to do,
Then you'll soon be good as new!"

Now Doctor Kangaroo has done his best,
He hops home to have a rest.

Soon everyone is feeling well.
In fact they're feeling rather swell!

They shout "HOORAY!",
And throw their bandages away.

"Doctor Kangaroo is the best!" they say,
"Let's go and thank him right away!"

They find Doctor Kangaroo in bed.
He has a bandage on his head.

Poor Doctor Kangaroo!
What are we going to do?

But Doctor Kangaroo says,
"There's nothing wrong with me -
It's my bedtime, don't you see?
And I always go to bed
With a bandage on my head!"

The end

(Or is it? . . .)

Little Lizard's bumped his head.
He doesn't want to go to bed!
So he doesn't call for Doctor Kangaroo -

He calls for Doctor Rhinoceros instead!

The end

(Really!)

More silly rhyming picture books
by Gerald Hawksley:

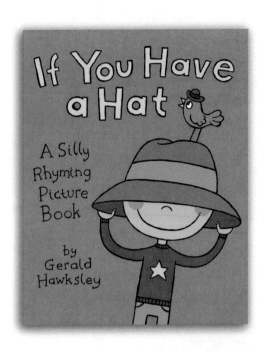

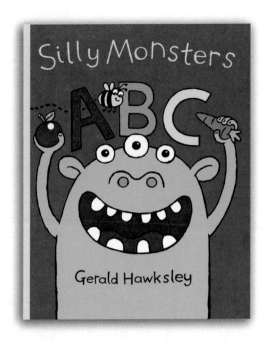

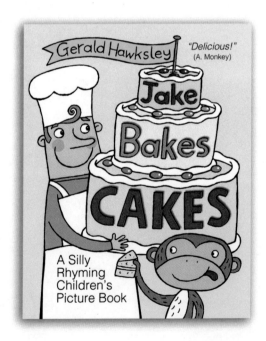

www.geraldhawksley.com

Made in the USA
Monee, IL
11 November 2022

17536901R00021